JADA JONES

★ DANCING QUEEN ★

JADA JONES
★ DANCING QUEEN ★

by Kelly Starling Lyons
illustrated by Nneka Myers

Penguin Workshop

PENGUIN WORKSHOP
An Imprint of Penguin Random House LLC, New York

Text copyright © 2019 by Kelly Starling Lyons. Cover illustration copyright © 2019 by Vanessa Brantley Newton. Illustrations copyright © 2019 by Penguin Random House LLC. All rights reserved. Published by Penguin Workshop, an imprint of Penguin Random House LLC, New York. PENGUIN and PENGUIN WORKSHOP are trademarks of Penguin Books Ltd, and the W colophon is a registered trademark of Penguin Random House LLC.
Manufactured in China.

Visit us online at www.penguinrandomhouse.com.

Book design by Kayla Wasil.

Library of Congress Cataloging-in-Publication Data is available upon request.

ISBN 9781524790585 (paperback)   10 9 8 7 6 5 4 3 2
ISBN 9781524790592 (library binding)   10 9 8 7 6 5 4 3 2 1

For everyone who shows kindness and creates change where they are—KSL

Thanks to my family and friends that keep pushing me to do my best and to never give up when trying new things!—NM

Chapter One:
COUNCIL CREW

After school, most kids rush to buses and car pool. But every Tuesday, I dash to Ms. Flowers's room for student council. Stepping through her door, you can't help but stand a little taller. Black-and-white posters of people who made a difference smile at you from the walls: Supreme Court Justice Sonia Sotomayor, Congressman John Lewis, mathematician Katherine Johnson, architect Maya Lin, and scientist Ernest Everett Just.

Each one has yellow silk roses

around their face. That's for friendship. Before they were change-makers, Ms. Flowers says, they were somebody's friend. Just like us.

"Welcome, Jada," she said with a grin as bright as her sunny classroom.

"Hi, Ms. Flowers," I called back.

Ms. Flowers always wears a blazer on top of a T-shirt that makes you think. Today's was stop-sign red and said: "Make Someone's Day." I spotted my buddy Miles and plopped onto a chair next to him. I love that we get to be in student council together. At first, he was an alternate for my class. But when a kid in another room had too many activities and asked to step down, Miles got his spot.

Student council president Chelsea Diaz, a fifth-grader, opened the meeting.

"The PTA thanks us for helping with the penny drive," she said. "The money we raised will go to our school field trip fund. For our next fund-raiser, let's think of something else that will make a big difference. Let's start with the suggestion box."

It was my turn to read the week's ideas. I flipped open the shoebox covered in Brookside colors of silver and blue and saw just one note at the bottom. I unfolded the sheet of notebook paper, and my heart sank as I read: *It's getting cold and I could use a new coat. Actually, my little brother could, too. Do you think student council could work on that?*

I thought about Raleigh. It doesn't snow like crazy like my mom's hometown of Syracuse, but some days are freezing. Mom told me that when she was little, her church collected and bought coats each year for people who needed them. Her family donated what they could. And

one year, it was my mom and Uncle Rob who were picking new coats for themselves from the giving closet.

"What if we had a drive called 'Coats for Caring'?" I said. "We could raise money to buy coats and give them to kids who need them here and in the community."

"Great idea, Jada!" Chelsea said.

"I like that, too," Miles said. "What if we had a 'Caring Week,' where everyone is reminded to show kindness?"

Ms. Flowers beamed at us like a proud parent.

"That's the spirit!" she said. "Jada, I really like your idea. Along with raising money to buy coats, students and parents could bring in gently used ones, too. How are

you going to inspire caring acts?"

"We could pass out kindness bingo boards for kids in kindergarten," a third-grader named Justice said.

"And checklists for older ones," another student added.

Chelsea nodded as the secretary took notes. She walked over to the whiteboard and grabbed a black dry-erase marker.

"Okay, what's our fund-raiser going to be?"

She wrote our ideas down as we fired them off: Mile run. Cookie sales. Family night at restaurants. They were all good, but we'd been there, done that. We needed something fun and fresh.

"How about a dance?" Miles said.

As fast as kids rushing to the floor when a good song comes on, a buzz filled the room. Everyone nodded and whispered. Some showed off moves in their seats. It was a great idea, so why did I feel queasy? I chewed on my bottom lip as my stomach churned.

"Love that!" Chelsea said. "Ms. Flowers, what do you think? Could we have a dance? We could sell tickets, snacks, and yellow tissue-paper roses for friendship."

"Sounds like you have a winner," Ms. Flowers said with a wink. "Instead of selling tickets, let's have donation boxes at the entrance. That way, everyone can go and just give if they can. We could also make up a list of fun dances and send pledge sheets home. People could donate money for each dance a student tries for an entire song."

Around the room, students nudged each other and bounced in excitement. To close the meeting, we formed a circle, and Chelsea led us in our chant.

"The Council Crew!"

"It's what we do!"

"The Council Crew!"

"It's what we do!"

"The Council Crew!"

"It's what we do!"

I grinned as I said goodbye to my buddies, but inside I groaned. Dancing with my besties Lena and Simone was cool, but trying out moves in front of everyone didn't sound like fun to me. Sometimes my mind thinks one thing and my feet do another. But helping friends was what mattered most. I took a breath and let it out slowly. How hard could it be?

Chapter Two: DANCE FEVER

Monday, when we opened the door to the gym, I knew the news was out. Music boomed and thumped like a party. Instead of starting warm-up exercises, Mr. Best grinned, spun around, and slid his feet from side to side.

"Go, Mr. B! Go, Mr. B!" kids cheered and danced along.

"Okay," he said, laughing.

"Everybody take a seat around the circle. I have exciting news. In less than two weeks, we're having a dance to raise money for coats for kids who need them. There will be a challenge, too: ten dances for you to try. The more you do, the more money you raise."

"All right!"

"Yes!"

Miles and his best friend RJ high-fived. Simone looked at me and Lena and grinned. I knew what she was thinking. They loved to jump rope and had moves like dancers on TV. I stared at the shiny wooden floor.

"Today, we're changing gym class to dance class to kick off the fun," Mr. Best said. Soon, the sounds of the line dance the Cupid Shuffle echoed in the room.

"Follow me."

Mr. Best led us through the steps, one at a time. Walking to the right, I could do that. Walking to the left, okay. Kicking then walking and turning. This wasn't so bad. But when it was time to put it all together, that's when things fell apart. Every time the line turned, I was a beat behind. I bumped into someone. I tripped over my feet. I was lost. I moved to the back and hoped nobody caught my stumbles. Thankfully, the

bell rang and set me free.

Simone and Lena didn't seem to notice.

"You know we have to do the challenge together," Simone said.

"Yeah," Lena said. "This is going to be awesome."

I smiled and nodded even though my head was throbbing. They were my best friends, but no way could I keep up with them. What was I going to do?

In class, Miss Taylor passed out the kindness checklists and pledge sheets. The more sponsors we signed up and dances we tried, the more money we could raise. No one would keep track of what dances

we completed. It was up to us to be honest.

I scanned the list of dances the Council Crew came up with: the Cupid Shuffle, Whip and Nae Nae, Chicken Dance, the Floss. It went on and on. As I read each one, I felt the jitters jamming in my stomach.

After school, I finished my homework and then started working on my poster for Caring Week.

Everyone on the Council Crew was making them to hang up in the hallway. I drew a pair of sneakers on a piece of yellow construction paper and wrote beneath it in bubble letters: *Put yourself in someone else's shoes.*

I thought back to the note I read in the meeting. I wondered who wrote it. What if it were Jackson and me who needed new coats? Tough times happen to everybody.

I remembered a couple years back when Daddy was laid off and looking for a new job. There wasn't money for extras.

I would do whatever I could to help raise money for coats, even if I had to dance with everyone watching. I found the Cupid Shuffle song and tried the moves again.

"What are you doing?" my little brother Jackson asked, standing in the doorway to my room. "You look funny. Want me to show you how?"

He moved to the right, to the left, kicked, walked and turned in time with the beat. I couldn't believe it. Not one mess-up. Not one missed step. He did the dance like he knew it his whole life.

"Where did you learn that?" I asked.

"In gym class."

My heart dropped. Jax could do the dance, but I couldn't. This just wasn't my day.

Chapter Three:
FAMILY JAM

At dinner, Jax spilled the beans. "Jada can't do the Cupid Shuffle."

"What?" Mom said. "Sure she can. We did it at the reunion, remember? We'll practice after we eat."

Great. Now I was a family project. It didn't help that my mom loves dancing. She does Zumba, takes African dance classes, can dance the

merengue and salsa. After we cleaned up the kitchen, it was time for Momma's Living Room Rhythm Studio. Ugh.

She hit the music.

"Follow me," she said. She started by breaking down the moves slowly. Baby steps. I could do that, but then we put it all together in real time. It was over.

I tried, but every time, I was a beat behind, like when you're trying to swat a fly and you just miss it.

Mom changed to a new song—one of her old-school classics.

"Let's just work on the beat first," she said.

She moved her feet back and forth with the music. Then, she added her arms and started bopping her head. I frowned as I tried to follow her lead.

"You're getting it," she said, smiling.

Were we seeing the same thing?

"Thanks, Mom," I said. "Can we do more later? I have some work to do."

I headed to my room and flopped onto my bed. I reached for my backpack and pulled out the checklist of kindness ideas. Caring Week didn't officially start for a few more days, but I was ready to start now.

One suggestion caught my eye: Invite someone new to sit with you at lunch or play at recess. I could do that. It wasn't that long ago when my BFF Mari moved away. I knew how it felt to want a friend.

"Hey, baby girl," Dad said, walking into my room. "You know I'm not the dancing type either. Want to know my secret?"

He didn't wait for my answer. Daddy put on his I-mean-business face, rocked back and forth, and did a move that made me look like a dancing queen.

"Don't worry about what everybody else is doing. Just do you."

I pressed my lips together to keep from smiling. Held in my stomach. Blinked as my eyes crinkled. Finally, my laugh burst like water through a dam and spilled into my room. It felt good to let it out, but dancing at home was one thing. Dancing in front of the whole school was another.

"Thanks, Daddy,"

I said. "I just don't want everyone staring at me. I'll figure it out."

"I know you will. You always do. But we're here if you need us."

At school the next morning, Lena couldn't wait until I sat down at our table.

"When do you want to get together to practice?" she said.

I shrugged.

"How about Saturday?"

"I'm not sure. I think we might be busy."

"Sunday?"

"I think we have something going on that day, too."

I knew I couldn't dodge her and Simone forever. What was I going to do?

Miss Taylor read a picture book to us during English Language Arts called *Each Kindness*. It was by one of my favorite authors, Jacqueline Woodson. In the story, a new girl is treated unfairly by her classmates. I shook my head when they ignored her. The line about how kindness spreads stayed with me all day: "Each little thing we do," their teacher said, "goes out, like a ripple, into the world."

I hoped our coat drive would help everyone in the school who needed one. I wanted our friends to be warm and know we cared.

Later, I stood near Miles in the lunch line. "I keep thinking about

that note I read in student council,"
I said.

"Me too," he replied. "I'm glad
we're helping."

We took our trays to our table and

sat next to our friends. I nibbled on my chicken nuggets and wondered if I would be brave enough to leave a note like that. I wondered if the writer was someone I knew.

At recess, I was hoping Lena and Simone would teach me a double Dutch trick I'd been wanting to learn. But when I heard music and saw speakers set up outside, I had a feeling they'd have other plans.

"That's what I'm talking about," Simone said, grooving to the beat.

Some of the boys were dancing, too. Miles and Carson were doing the Floss. Gabi did the Sprinkler.

"Let's see what you got, Jada," Simone said.

I frowned and tried to remember the steps Mom showed me. I moved my feet and nodded my head. My braids hit me in the face. I felt as stiff as a robot. Why couldn't this be easy?

"You're thinking about it too much," Simone said. "Just relax."

I tried, but I just couldn't move like her and Lena. They looked good without even trying. I wished my feet would do what I wanted, but it was like they had their own brain.

"You guys have fun," I said. "I'm taking a break."

I sat on the browning grass and listened to the music and the sounds

of my friends laughing. They were loving the recess dance party. Was I the only one who wasn't excited?

Then I saw a girl from another class sitting down, too. She was wearing a hooded jean jacket with colorful patches and gazing at the sky. She didn't have anyone next to her. I got up and moved closer.

"You're not a dancer either," I said.

"You don't want to see me," she said, laughing, and pointed at her faded red flats. "Two left feet. You're Jada, right? I remember when you gave that speech when you were running for student council. Pretty cool. I'm Hallie."

"I've seen you around. Nice to

meet you. Maybe we could work on
our not-so-cool moves together."

She laughed at that.

We talked until our teachers
called us to line up for our classes.
We had so much in common. We both

had little brothers, couldn't dance,
liked science.

"See you later, twin," she said.

I smiled and walked to my class.

"Where did you go?" Lena asked
when I got in line.

"I was talking to a friend," I said, looking over at Hallie.

"Don't worry about the dance challenge," Simone said. "We'll help you."

I sighed. If only that would be enough.

Chapter Four:
THE SCIENCE OF DANCE

Practicing on my own wasn't helping. Dancing with family and friends was a fail. I needed a secret weapon. When Mom asked if I wanted to come with her to the Richard B. Harrison Library, an idea zapped me like a shock. Why hadn't I thought of this before?

Richard B. was one of my favorite places. Had to be something there

that could help. As we walked back
to Mom's department—the children's
section—I waved at everyone behind
the front desk.

"Hey, Jada," they called.

While Mom worked on a new display, I searched for inspiration.

I flipped through books about dance. My shoulders slumped when nothing clicked. It was hopeless. I decided to check out science and technology books, since those always made me smile. I read until I saw something I couldn't believe. I sat up straight— did I read that right? *Motion-controlled video games may help improve real-life skills.* I felt the zap of an idea strike me again. What if they could help with dancing?

"I'm all done," Mom said. "Ready?"

I jumped up and nodded. Usually, I want to stay and find new books to check out, but today I headed right for the door. I couldn't wait to put my hypothesis to the test.

Mom did workout videos or grooved along with video games like *Just Dance* when she didn't have time for a class. I turned on the game and tried to match the steps of the avatar dancers. I wasn't on beat and my moves were off, but at least now I could see what I was doing wrong. I broke into a sweat as I tried again and again. As I practiced, my moves slowly started getting more in sync.

"Go, Jada!" Mom said when she walked into the room.

Before I knew it, I was smiling. For the first time since the dance was announced, I felt a little better. Maybe I wouldn't be a dancing dud after all.

Chapter Five:
A FRIEND IN NEED

"It's going to be a cold one today," Mom said to me and Jax on Monday morning. "Make sure you wear your heavy jackets and take your gloves."

Outside, tiny crystals of ice dotted our car's windshield. I watched them melt as Mom defrosted the window and wondered what I would do if I didn't have a warm coat to wear.

At school, I walked Jax to kindergarten and saw the back of a familiar jean jacket on the way to my class. I waved at Hallie when she turned around, but she didn't see me. She hurried into her room.

Miss Taylor switched on the school's morning news. I smiled when I saw Simone's face on the TV screen. She was one of the announcers that day.

"Good morning, Brookside," she said, clear and cheerful. "Today is the beginning of Caring Week. It's all about being extra kind to each other. And don't forget to practice for the big dance on Friday. Are you ready for the challenge? I know I am."

Classes cheered as the music for "Watch Me (Whip/Nae Nae)" played. Simone and her cohost nailed the dances. From their seats, kids joined in. Caring Week was on.

As I walked down the hall, I saw bins where people could donate coats. There were already a few in there, and this was just the first day. It would be amazing if we raised lots of money to buy some, too. I hoped whoever put the note in the suggestion box would get a new coat soon.

We had indoor recess since it was so cold outside. As we played Uno, I told Simone and Lena about my video game dance practice.

"That's cool, Jada," Simone said. "Don't forget to try the dances on the challenge list, so you're ready. Can you practice this week?"

I nodded but felt the worries creeping up again. The dance was just days away. I wanted to raise as much money as I could, but having to do ten whole dances? Whew. In my living room, it was just the screen and me. In the school gym, everyone would be there. I tried to shut out the doubts and focus on the good we were doing.

I smiled as I thought about the kindness I saw spreading through the school. Kids let classmates get in front of them in line, gave one another compliments, and offered to help teachers. It seemed like everyone was making new friends.

At the end of the day when I went to my cubby to get my puffy purple jacket, Miles put my chair up on my desk for me. I asked Miss Taylor if she wanted me to erase her whiteboard before I headed home. Caring was contagious.

On the way down the hall, I saw Hallie and was just about to catch up to her and say hi when something hit me. I remembered the ice on our car window. Was it still as cold outside? Hallie just had on her jean jacket. Didn't she say she had a little brother? I felt a familiar jolt as a thought snapped into my mind: Was she the one who wrote the note?

Chapter Six:
DIGGING DEEP

At home in my room, I thought about Hallie. I didn't know for sure that she needed a coat, but someone did. I looked at my pledge sheet. Mom, Dad, my uncle Rob, and my babysitter were

PLEDGE

mom _____

Dad _____

Uncle Rob _____

Kayla _____

already sponsoring me. I had to work harder.

I picked up the phone and called my pop pop.

"Hey, Lady Bug," he said when he heard my voice. I smiled at his special name for me.

"We're doing a ten-dance challenge at school to raise money to buy coats for kids," I said. "Would you be one of my sponsors?"

"Sure," he said. "Sounds like a great cause. How does it work?"

After I filled him in, Pop Pop pledged one dollar for each dance I completed.

I thanked him and wrote his name on my sheet. With pledges

from fifty cents to one dollar per dance, I felt good about the money I was raising. But I knew I could do more.

I looked at my dragon bank. I had been saving up for a rock tumbler for months. It would make the rough stones in my collection shine like gems. But this was much more important.

I twisted open the bottom. Coins tinkled as they spilled onto my desk. I reached inside and pulled out the dollars, too. I counted the money—quarters, dimes, nickels, pennies. They all added up. I counted again just to be sure. I had forty-one dollars and fifty-one cents. Was that enough?

"Mom, can we please go to the store after dinner?" I asked and filled her in on what I wanted to do.

She gave me a hug.

I headed right for the girls' department when we got there. I saw racks of coats and wasn't sure how to choose. There were sleek ones, fuzzy ones, long ones, short ones, all different shades. I finally decided to pick something I would love to give a friend. I found a fluffy light blue jacket with a furry hood. It was warm and soft. Cute, too. I flipped over the price tag and put my head down. It was twice what I had.

"How much is it, Jada?" Mom asked.

She looked at the cost and put the coat in the cart.

"It will make someone really happy," she said. "Your dad and I will pay the difference."

The next morning, I dropped the new coat in the bin. I was glad it had warmed up and we could have recess outside again. I found Hallie and invited her to jump rope with Simone, Lena, Carson, and me. She missed and tripped a few times, but

she didn't care. She smiled and kept going. Seeing her reminded me of Daddy. I could hear his voice in my head. "Don't worry about what everybody else is doing. Just do you."

"Are you ready for the dance?" I asked as we waited for our next turn.

"I guess."

"Let's do it together," I said.

"Watch out, feet, here we come," she said, laughing.

After school, it was our last student council meeting before the big event. Everyone was pumped.

"Our coat drive is going great," Chelsea said. "We have coats for kids and adults. The PTA will put out bins on dance night, too. We have volunteers to sell snacks and the tissue-paper roses. We're almost there."

We all clapped, smiling at one another.

"Caring Week ends Friday, but I know we'll keep showing kindness all year long. I'm proud of all of you, of our school," Ms. Flowers said. Today's T-shirt was night-sky black and, in rainbow colors that twinkled like fireworks, read: "Be the Change."

I knew I wouldn't be the same when this was over. It started with one wish for a coat and turned into so much more.

Chapter Seven:

ON THE FLOOR

The Council Crew helped set up the gym for the dance. We decorated it with silver and blue balloons and a matching banner. Signs around the room reminded everyone of our cause: Coats for Caring. When we finished, I stood back and looked at the room. Wow. It was amazing to see our dream come true.

"This is going to be the best dance ever," Miles said, admiring it next to me.

I knew he was right.

When the doors opened, the crowd was ready. A friend's mom, DJ Smooth, worked her magic with the music. She had skills. The dance floor stayed full with all the hits and old-school classics she played.

I saw my dad selling snacks and ran over to say hi.

"You ready, baby girl?" he asked. "I know I am. Been saving some special moves just for today."

He put on his I-mean-business face. Uh-oh.

"Daddy, I have to find Lena and Simone."

He laughed.

I walked through the crowd.
There were so many people. Parents,
teachers, kids from different grades.
Friends bought yellow paper roses
for each other. I saw Jax and waved.
He waved back and jammed with his
buddies. Everywhere, people smiled
and danced.

"Okay, Brookside, are you ready
for the challenge?" DJ Smooth
screamed.

Just hearing those words froze
me to my spot. I gulped and backed
up to the wall. I wondered if I would
find the courage to get through it.
I had to. But I didn't know how. Then
I saw Hallie. She walked over to me

with a nervous smile.

"Ready to do this?" she asked.

"If you are?"

"Together."

We walked to the center of the floor, found Lena and Simone, and waited for the first song to start.

My heart pounded as I heard the beginning of the Cupid Shuffle. I took a breath. It was now or never.

I panicked and stumbled at first as the crowd moved in a line to the right. But after we got started, I stopped trying to get it perfect. It was

pretty fun when I stopped freaking out. I saw other kids missing a step or just going with the flow like Hallie and me. It didn't matter if you could do the dance like a pro, just that you tried. Just like that, it was over.

DJ Smooth called out the next move as a new song filled the room.

"Who can Floss?" she asked.

Hallie and I laughed as we tried to get the arm and hip moves coordinated. Maybe we could do it slowly. But fast like Simone? That was a lost cause. Before we knew it, that was over, too. The songs kept changing, with a new dance each time, playing for a minute or two before switching to the next.

When the last dance was over, we hugged and jumped up and down. We did it! I couldn't wait to find out how much money everybody raised.

But DJ Smooth wasn't finished.

"I know it's called the Ten-Dance Challenge," she said into the mike. "But I'm throwing in one more—an oldie but goodie. Let's see what you can do in the Soul Train line."

I saw some confused faces, but I knew just what she was talking about. My mom gets in the Soul Train line at every wedding reception, every reunion. It's a time to show off your special moves. I loved watching it, but no way was I joining in. Doing the dance challenge was a big enough step for me. Maybe I'd try a solo dance next time.

Simone and Lena raced to the line. So did Miles, Carson, Gabi, and Jax.

"You sure you don't want to try it?" Hallie said.

I scrunched my eyebrows and shook my head.

"Together?"

I thought about the week of caring and what really mattered. This was about having fun and celebrating one another. Maybe it was time to try something new. I smiled and got in line.

I noticed something as I watched my friends dance down the middle: No one's moves were just the same.

Some were jerky. Others were silly, flashy, flowing. Everybody had their own style. When it was our turn, Hallie and I danced just like we wanted. We waved our arms and did a double high five, then spun and strutted down the line.

"Go, Jada! Go, Hallie!" I heard my friends chant.

I don't know how we looked, but who cares? We were having fun. Doing us. Together.

Chapter Eight:
A NEW GROOVE

At school the next week, we found out that we raised more than four thousand dollars for coats and collected more than one hundred gently used ones. A local store learned what we were doing and donated hats and gloves. We even had enough to share with a couple other schools, too.

Something else happened.

Though Caring Week was over, someone put a card in my cubby that said: *You're awesome.* I saw older kids tying the shoelaces of kindergartners. Kids invited new friends to sit with them at lunch. I remembered the ripple of kindness from the book my teacher read to us during English Language Arts. It just kept spreading and growing.

At recess, Hallie had on a new jacket. It was just like my puffy purple one, but hers was red.

"Now we're really twins," I said.

"Yep," she said, smiling.

I couldn't wait to get to student council. As soon as the bell rang, I rushed to Ms. Flowers's room. On the

way there, I saw a light blue fluffy
coat with a furry hood. My heart
jumped. Was it the one I bought?
I smiled to myself and didn't try to
see who it was.

When I stepped into Ms. Flowers's room, I saw something new on her "Made a Difference" wall. There was a picture of the Council Crew surrounded by yellow roses. I just kept staring at it. It was the best gift I ever saw.

"That's us," I said in shock when she came over.

"Yes, Jada," Ms. Flowers said, wearing a sky-blue T-shirt with the shimmering words "Dream and Do." "Each of you earned a spot on my wall. I'm so proud."

I sat next to Miles and pointed to the picture.

"Can you believe it?"

"I know. It's awesome."

He held up his fist. I bumped it with mine.

"We did it!" Chelsea said when she opened the meeting. "Now, how are we going to top that?"

We laughed. It was Miles's turn to read the comments in the suggestion box. He flipped it open and pulled out the notes inside. A couple asked about having more fun activities like dances. Another one suggested a field trip to the beach. But one folded piece of notebook paper just said, "Thank you."

That one meant the most to all of us there.

"Let's end with our chant," Chelsea said.

We got into a circle and smiled at each other.

"The Council Crew!" Chelsea yelled.

"It's what we do!" we answered.

"The Council Crew!"

"It's what we do!"

"The Council Crew!"

"It's what we do!"

Each of us stretched out our hands and piled them one on top of another. I wasn't sure what challenge we'd face next, but I knew we could do anything. We were friends and change-makers.

JADA'S RULES FOR BEING A DANCING QUEEN

1. Move to the beat of your heart.

2. Relax and let it flow.

3. Tell your doubts to get out of the way.

4. Have fun.

5. Find your groove with friends.

ACKNOWLEDGMENTS

Thank you to the brilliant Penguin Workshop team, illustrators Nneka Myers and Vanessa Brantley Newton, my agent Caryn Wiseman, my family, and the many friends who cheered me on, gave me feedback, and spread the word about Jada Jones. Special shout-outs to: Tanesha Taylor Nurse, Olugbemisola Rhuday-Perkovich, Debbi Michiko Florence, Laura Pegram, Doni Kay, my sands and sorors, Brown Bookshelf fam, Novelette sisters, and the AACC crew.